The Vampire's Special Grizzly

ASPHALT BAY PACK BOOK 10

EZRA DAWN

The Vampire's Special Grizzly
Ezra Dawn

Cover art created by JeB Designs
jebdesigns@outlook.com

Table of Contents

Other Books by Ezra Dawn

Contact the Author

Character Name
Pronunciation

Alaric Glazkov (Ah-lar-ic, Glaz-kov)

Teagan Spade (Tea-gan, Spade)

(This story is part of an interconnecting series that was written with the intention of being read in a certain order.)

Alaric Glazkov is the vampire drummer for the band The Dead Tuesdays by night and a video game programmer by day. After aiding in the battle against the dark coven, life is getting back to normal for him and the rest of his friends. The only problem? He's the last single guy in their group. Feeling like the tenth wheel whenever they go out, Alaric longs for someone to call his own now that meaningless sex is no longer doing it for him.

Teagan Spade is a grizzly bear shifter and former special forces operative turned council guardsman. Tasked with protecting two councilmen, Teagan accompanied Krealik and Valik into battle. Now that the fight is over and the councilmen are settled with their mates and staying close to Asphalt Bay, a place full of mated couples, Teagan is faced with his own loneliness.

When an overzealous fan from the past resurfaces Alaric decides to hire a bodyguard and Teagan comes highly recommended by Councilman Krealik. When the two men learn they're mates, the realize there's more at stake than they thought.

Vozlyublennyy – Russian for Beloved

Hekili – Hawaiian for Thunder

This book is part of an interconnecting series with a villain plot that spans multiple books! It was written with the intention that the books would be read in a certain order. If you start from this one, you'll be confused! Below is the correct reading order.

1. An Alpha for the Demigod (Asphalt Bay One)

2. The Enforcer's Secret Vampire (Asphalt Bay Two)

3. The Beta's Poison Bite (Asphalt Bay Three)

4. Taming the Feral Tiger (Asphalt Bay Four)

5. The Alpha's Master (Venetian Hills One)

6. The Second's Cursed Mate (Venetian Hills Two)

7. The Doctor's Demon Prince (Asphalt Bay Five)

8. The Leopard's Twin Troubles (Asphalt Bay Six)

9. The Beta's Second Chance (Venetian Hills Three)

10. The Panther's Favorite Bully (Venetian Hills Four)

11. The Warlock's Beautiful Bird (Asphalt Bay Seven)

Alaric

Prologue

Fifty Years Ago...

Entering the courtroom, I sit in the back pew closest to the door so I can leave once the verdict is read and get back on the road with the guys. We're supposed to be playing a show in Amsterdam tonight and will have to hurry to make it on time. My friends wanted to be here for moral support, but I told them I wanted to do this alone. They sat through the entire trial with me and that was enough. When we started this journey as bandmates I didn't think about the craziness that comes with being famous. Sure, we're only famous to paranormals, so we don't have paparazzi following our every move just to get a picture of something they can sell to tabloids. Which is a blessing. No, our problem is overzealous fans. We've all had our share of weirdos, but it's never gone this far before.

It started innocent enough with Angelo wanting an autograph and a picture that I was happy to give. Angelo was a flirt but not my type, so I never took him up on what he was offering. He started appearing at every show and I'd run into him at random places while I was out and about on my off days. It started happening so often I couldn't chalk it up to coincidence anymore. Then bodies started dropping and brought investigators to my door thinking I was responsible for the deaths of every one-night stand I'd had since I met Angelo.

I didn't know what to think when I was brought into an interrogation room and left there to sweat for hours before council investigators came in to speak to me. One of them was a wolf shifter so they knew I was telling the truth when I said I had nothing to do with the crimes committed. Still, they wanted to know if I had any idea why the men I slept with were being targeted. At first, I didn't have an answer for them. It was when they showed me pictures of the crime scenes and I saw the words 'he's mine' written in their blood on the walls that I considered Angelo might be involved.

I didn't want to believe someone so seemingly harmless, and innocent could be capable of such brutality, but the signs were there. Stalkers have been known to escalate to violence whenever someone or something threatens the fantasy they've built. Usually, it's the object of their obsession that becomes the target in the end but the people around them can easily be targets too. It all came to a head after a warrant for Angelo's arrest was issued and I was set free.

I'd gotten to my hotel room to find Angelo waiting for me. We fought, he got the upper hand when he injected me with some kind of drug, and I was down for the count. When I came to it was to find Angelo tied up and gagged in the corner being watched like a hawk by friends. They'd heard the commotion and came to my rescue before Angelo could do anything to me.

Angelo was arrested and here we are. The sound of a gavel hammering draws my attention to the front of the room where a council judge is about to announce his verdict.

"Angelo Romanov, for the crimes you've committed I sentence you to a hundred years in solitary confinement in a council penitentiary. After which you will be executed. You don't deserve an easy death after what you've done, and I won't be giving it to you. Court adjourned."

Shoulders sagging in relief, I stand and leave the courtroom. *It's over.*

Alaric

Chapter 1

Rolling out of bed, I scrub my hands over my face and stroll naked into the bathroom to take care of my morning routine. My head is pounding telling me I had too many of those flaming green shots at the Blue Moon last night. My friends are all mated off and being the last single guy in the group makes me feel like a tenth wheel whenever we go out. Last night was no different. I'm lonelier than I've ever been and desperate for what my friends have. I've given up on one-night stands because my dick and I stopped taking an interest in anyone.

I keep spending my nights getting drunk enough to forget my feelings and my days losing myself in work. I'm a software engineer that specializes in video game development and I've been working on a new MMORPG. I've based the game around Norse mythology. The people playing the game will pick an avatar from one of the nine worlds to start their journey. They'll have to complete quests, collect items, and beat the world boss in order to unlock the next world and continue the storyline. They'll have three tries to beat the final boss. After those three attempts, Ragnarök will destroy the world and they'll have to start over from the beginning.

After five years of development, the game is finally ready to go through the testing stage where I'll fix any issues. Once it's ready for launch, I'll shop it around to gaming companies and sell it to the highest bidder. I consider myself a freelance developer. I don't work for any one specific gaming company. Instead, I develop the games I get ideas for and sell them while also taking on temporary developing jobs from different companies when they interest me.

Being almost five hundred years old, I don't need the money, but I'm not the type to sit around and twiddle my thumbs so I keep working. Video game development has been something I dabbled in since its inception. Of the many jobs I've held in my lifetime, creating something from a simple idea like I do with my games is by far my favorite. Playing music is a close second. I've got a whole team of beta testers I hired going over Enemy of Valhalla. They'll report any issues to me when they're done, so I'll be working on a couple projects I've been hired for in the meantime.

After brushing my teeth, I step into the shower to wash off my night so I can start my day. When I get out, I head back into the bedroom where I grab a t-shirt and a pair of athletic shorts from my dresser. Putting them on, I go downstairs to the kitchen. Walking over to the coffee pot, I pour myself a cup of from the freshly brewed pot and take a sip, enjoying the bitter taste of it. Now that my cup is full, I grab a bag of blood from the fridge and empty half the contents into the carafe, then swish it around to mix it into the coffee before putting the carafe back.

I tend to drink coffee all day while I'm working so I mix blood into it. I don't enjoy the taste of the bagged stuff. The additives that keep it from coagulating change the flavor. So, I mask it with coffee. Normally, I get my blood from my one-night stands but since I haven't had any of those lately, I've had to switch to the bagged stuff. I could probably go to Venetian Hills and see if the coven there would let me feed from one of their donors but it's not worth the hassle.

Setting my cup down, I pull ingredients for an omelet from the fridge and get to work cooking myself breakfast. This house is too fucking quiet now that the guys have all moved into their own houses, so I turn on my echo dot and say, "Alexa, play my 'fill the silence' playlist." As *Alter Bridge's Addicted to Pain* blares through the kitchen, I start chopping the veggies that'll go into my omelet. If I didn't want a family someday, I'd find somewhere else to live that isn't as big as this place.

I've thought about advertising for a roommate but after the shit with Angelo, I'm not about to invite a stranger into my space for longer than it takes to get off a few times. While I know the things Angelo did weren't my fault I can't help feeling like it is. For years, I've gone over everything I did or said to him trying to figure out if I inadvertently led him on somehow. Drove myself crazy with it until Mishka, Kira, and Altair convinced me to get help. It took putting myself in therapy for me to realize that the simplest gestures could spark a delusion in someone like Angelo.

I had to come to terms with the fact that all it would take is a smile or a kind word and I'd become the center of someone's obsession. In Angelo's head, even though we were complete strangers we were in a relationship and anyone I ever slept with became a threat to that relationship he had to eliminate. I thank the gods every day that I never met my beloved during the time Angelo was free because if I had, who knows what would've happened. *Quit trying to fool yourself, Alaric. You know exactly what would've happened.* Angelo would've killed my beloved and I would've died too. And to Angelo, having me dead would've been better than letting someone else have me.

I really need to stop thinking about this. It's been fifty years since Angelo was sentenced and I have got to move on from it. You'd think it'd be easy but it's not. Truth is, the whole thing fucked me up. I quit having sex with anyone and stopped interacting with fans for years. Once I started therapy, that all changed but the guilt over the deaths of my former bed partners still lingers to this day. I live with the fear that someone else is going to latch on to me like Angelo did and because of it, I don't let anyone get close to me. Even when I'm with a one-night stand, I keep them at a distance. They might know my name, but I refuse to get theirs. Any conversation we have pertains to what our preferences are in the bedroom and when they leave, it's with the knowledge they'll never see me again. And if they decided to darken my doorstep again in hopes of a repeat performance, they'd surely regret it.

I could use mind control to make them forget my address, but I consider that to be an abuse of power, so I don't do it. Finishing my breakfast, I rinse my plate and stick it in the dishwasher with the other dishes I used. Polishing off my coffee, I fix myself another cup and take it into the living room where I left my laptop yesterday. Since the guys moved out, I've quit holing myself up in my room whenever I'm working. It made me feel like too much of a recluse since I'm here alone, so now I work from anywhere in the house.

Grabbing the computer and my Bluetooth earbuds, I tell Alexa to pause on my way out to the back porch. Leaving my mug on the table next to the hammock, I climb onto it, and open my laptop. Once it boots up, I pop my earbuds in, hit play on my 'you better work' playlist and dive into the first coding job I need to finish. There's a nice breeze blowing making the hammock sway. We're in the middle of Spring, so we aren't at the point where the temperature outside is sweltering hot yet. Meaning I can enjoy working out here in comfort. The back porch has a roof on it, so I don't have to worry about the sun making me sick if I sit out here during the day. Otherwise, I'd have to sit under an umbrella curled like a pretzel to make sure the sun doesn't touch any part of me.

Sometimes I wish sun sickness had a cure but it's a vampire's Achilles' heel and nothing can be done about it. It's something we have to live with. Most vampires sleep during the day and come out at night, but I'm not one of them. I should probably get more sleep than I actually do, but four to six hours is enough for me. Occasionally, I'll have a nightmare about the past and will only get two hours of sleep.

Sometimes less. Makes coffee my lifeline because I'm a zombie the day after a nightmare. Thankfully, the nightmares are few and far between now. It was hell when they were a nightly occurrence, but therapy and time has helped to curb them. I have faith that soon I won't have to deal with them anymore.

After a few hours of work, my computer pings with a reminder. The computer is linked to my phone so any texts, notifications, and phone calls will come through on it since I usually can't hear it ring when I have my earbuds in.

```
Tattoo Appointment at 2:30
today.
```

Shit, I'd forgotten about that. Saving my work, I shut down my laptop and head inside. I'm getting my first tattoo today. I've changed my mind on what I want multiple times, so it took a while for me to finally decide otherwise I'd have gotten a tattoo before now. I stumbled across one online that called to me on a deep level. I felt it in my soul that this was the one. It's going on my chest and will be of a grizzly bear with a forest and mountain scene inside the body and birds flying above it. I don't understand what led me to it, but my gut feelings have never steered me wrong before so I'm rolling with it.

Leaving my laptop in the living room, I pull on a pair of shoes, stuff my phone into my pocket, and don my sunglasses. On my way out the door, I grab my keys and wallet from the entry table and head to my truck. It's a solid black short bed Dodge Ram quad cab with a lift kit. The windows are tinted dark to protect me from the sunlight. Add in the black rims on the tires and the damn thing looks mean. I love it. When I drove it off the lot at the dealership, I was happier than a pig in shit and driving it never fails to bring a smile to my face. These days, I get my happiness any way I can because it helps take my mind off how unhappy and lonely I really am. Climbing in my truck, I start the engine, input the address of the tattoo parlor in my GPS and let Morgan Freeman tell me where to go.

Chapter 2

Walking into the council offices, I enter the first open elevator and scan my key card. The panel hiding the underground floor buttons opens and I press the one that'll take me to the second underground floor where the training area is. The paranormal council building is made up of seven floors. Three above, four below. The first floor is the lobby and clerical offices. Second floor houses the courtrooms and offices of the council's judges. The top floor is where the councilmen and women have their offices and courtroom.

The council members don't oversee every single case that comes through here. The judges handle a lot of them and the council only steps in to make a ruling on their cases when asked. Since they're responsible for a huge chunk of the council's caseload. the judges are heavily vetted to ensure there's a slim chance of them being corrupted. No one wants to risk a criminal being set free when every shred of evidence points to them being deserving of a jail cell.

Not all paranormals can scent lies and it's considered discriminatory to only employ wolf shifters as judges. Besides, if there's corruption involved, it won't matter if the person's guilt is confirmed by someone who can scent lies or not. The judge's word is final on a case and if they decide to rule in favor of the prisoner and not the prosecution despite overwhelming evidence thanks to a bribe, there's nothing we can do about it unless we appeal to the council and ask for a review of the judge's decision.

We might suspect corruption but if it can't be proven, we're shit out of luck so it's better to vet the judges instead of having to launch a full-on investigation into why they made the ruling they did. On the flip side, a corrupt judge with an agenda could easily put an innocent person behind bars because of some perceived slight or prejudice they might have.

The first underground floor houses the armory, panic rooms and security monitors that are watched by at least four guards 24/7. If the building ever comes under attack, there's a plan in place to get everyone down to the panic rooms using secret entrances from every floor above. It'll help keep the number of casualties to a minimum. The second floor is dedicated to training. It has every piece of gym equipment known to man along with obstacle courses a pool for water training, and even a dedicated all-terrain area complete with a forest, desert, and mountain. We use it when we don't have the time to get to the outdoor facility for a lengthy training mission.

I've been a personal guard to Councilmen Krealik and Valik for years now, but I like to keep my instincts sharp, so I come down here three times a week before my shift officially starts. Personal guards work on a rotation so there's one of us with each councilman at all times. I usually cover the night shift but one of the other guards met his mate recently. So the rest of us are pulling doubles to cover his shifts while he takes time off to bond.

We've been working so closely together for years we don't trust anyone else with the councilmen's protection. Bringing someone else in to cover for Matt was out of the question. If there's trouble the three of us can't handle by ourselves we'll call in the team that we keep stationed nearby. The team is one of many made up of council guards. They're usually the ones that are back-up whenever a council member travels but there's no way of knowing which team we'll get until it's time to go. Most of the teams have never seen a combat situation and while I know the council takes their training regimens seriously, I don't trust anyone whose instincts in battle haven't been tested by a true threat.

In the years I've been working for Krealik and Valik, they and the other three guards have become like family to me. Aside from the friends I call brothers from the time I spent in the military and my two sisters, they're all the family I've got left. My sleuth was wiped out by a wildfire years ago. They were trying to evacuate but a rockslide trapped them on the mountain. My younger sisters were away at college otherwise I would've lost them too. Lisa was at Harvard law while Theresa was at Vanderbilt's school of nursing. Both have graduated and gone into their chosen professions. Now that I'm based in Asphalt Bay with Krealik and Valik and commuting with them to the council buildings when they're needed here, my sisters have decided to move here to be closer to me.

I look forward to being able to see them more often. Right now, I'm lucky if I manage to make the trip once a month and half the time, I never get to see both of them together because their jobs are demanding, and they're based in two different cities. The sound of people training greets me when the elevator doors open and pulls me out of my thoughts. Stepping out, I turn left and make my way to the men's locker rooms. Everyone gets assigned a locker to use so there's enough lockers in here for a thousand men and twenty showers.

My nose wrinkles at the smell in here. I know paranormals have sensitive noses so spraying air freshener and using scented cleaners isn't something anyone likes to do but damn, something has to be done about this place. It smells like a mix of sweaty ass crack and balls and week-old dirty socks in here. *Disgusting.* Heading for my locker, I use my thumbprint and combination to unlock it then stash my stuff inside it. I knew I'd be training today so I came dressed for it. I'll shower and change into my usual tactical pants and black t-shirt before I report for duty.

I tape up my hands and grab my mouth guard before closing the locker. My mouth guard is custom made so I can speak and breathe easily with it. After double checking to be sure my locker's locked, I head into the training room. I've only got an hour, so I make my way over to the sparring mats where my friend Eric is waiting for me. I knew I'd be short on time this morning, so I arranged this sparring match last night. Stepping out of my boots, I take off my socks and tuck them inside them before inserting my mouth guard and walking onto the mat.

Krealik and Valik are only going to be in the building for half a day today before they have to depart for a meeting with the Alpha of the Coal Springs pack. They'll be getting an update on the rescued paranormals Coal Springs is housing after a lab was discovered and dismantled less than a half hour drive from their territory. As the head of Krealik and Valik's personal security, it's my job to arrange everything for their trip to ensure their safety. It'll take most of my morning to make sure everyone is up to speed on what to do if we come under attack and that we have all the supplies we'll need like comms, weapons, tracking devices and other tech. Most of the time, we don't need everything I pack but I live by the motto it's better to have it and not need it than to need it and not have it. I like to be prepared for anything.

The battle with the dark coven might be over but here we are, almost two years later, and we're still dismantling the labs they had set up and arresting the people still involved with them. Every time we think we've gotten the last one, more information comes in leading to another location we didn't know about. It seems like an endless fight, but I've got a feeling we're close to seeing the light at the end of the tunnel now. Word came in a week ago that the last international lab was found and destroyed so all that remains are the ones on this continent. The most recent lab raid revealed at least three more between Mexico and Canada so hopefully those will be the last.

Bouncing on the balls of my feet like a boxer, I shake my arms and move my head from side to side to loosen up. Eric does the same thing, then raises his hands in front of him. "Ready?"

Grinning, I nod. "Come at me bro."

Chapter 3

It's late by the time I leave the tattoo parlor. Instead of doing multiple sessions to complete the design I chose to sit through the entire thing. It took almost eight hours and even with my healing abilities kicking in my chest still feels like it's on fire with the sting. I scheduled this appointment to coincide with a night off from performing at the club. If I hadn't, the guys would be pissed at me by now because I'd be late as hell to our set.

My stomach is growling as I make my way across the parking lot to my truck. We took a break for food but that was hours ago and I'm starving. I'll have to stop at a fast-food place on the way home. When I get to my truck, a niggling sensation of being watched hits me. It's been happening a lot over the last week and I'm starting to get paranoid. Looking around, I don't see anyone except Vic locking up the tattoo parlor with a baby seat containing a sleeping infant at his feet. The man loves his son so much he brings him to work with him and even converted one of the empty booths in the shop into a nursery for him. With Vic busy working on me, his employees took turns taking care of the little guy.

Vic sees me watching him and waves before picking up the car seat and heading for the Jeep Wrangler parked nearby. The feeling of being watched is still there after he's gone. Shaking my head, I hit the unlock button on my keys and am surprised when I find the doors are already unlocked. Suspicious and on edge now, I open the door of my truck and curse when I see the black gift box tied with red ribbon on my seat. *Son of a bitch...not again.*

Moving the box, I climb into the truck and start the engine. Judging by the smell of blood coming from the box, I'm not going to like what's inside it when I open the damn thing. Putting the truck in gear, I pull out of the parking lot so fast the tires squeal. I break the speed limit all the way home, completely forgetting about stopping for food. When I enter the house, I zoom around making sure every door and window is locked and that the alarm is set. Satisfied the house is secure, I put the box on the kitchen counter and untie the ribbon. Hesitantly, I lift the lid on the box. Inside, nestled among dead

flowers is a heart with a knife in it. Attached to the
knife is a note.

YOU BETRAYED ME

Eyes wide, I stumble back from the box. *It can't
be. He's supposed to be in jail.* With shaking hands, I
pull my phone from my pocket and scroll through the
contacts until I find one I need. Hitting call on
councilman Krealik's number I wait for him to
answer while trying to tamp down the sudden need
to panic. He'll have access to the prison records and
can tell me if Angelo was released or not. Hopefully
he won't bite my head off too badly for calling him so
late.

Krealik answers with a growl, "This had better
be an emergency."

"Apologies for the late call Councilman. This is
Alaric Glazkov. I need your help."

"What can I do for you?"

"I just received a disturbing package that points
to someone from my past resurfacing. The problem
is, he's supposed to be serving the second half of a
one-hundred-year jail sentence in a council
penitentiary. I need to know if he was released early
despite the fact he's supposed to be executed once his

time is served or if he's still there and I'm dealing with someone else."

I hear Krealik moving followed by the sound of a computer booting up. "Alright, what's the name?"

"Angelo Romanov." I wait for him to search it. When he curses, I know he's got bad news for me.

"It looks like Angelo Romanov escaped custody two weeks ago. He pretended to be dead to lure the rookie guard into his cell where he got the upper hand, incapacitated the man, stole his uniform and walked right out of the prison. The council is in the process of updating all its prisons with facial recognition at the entrances to alert us if the person wearing the guard's uniform doesn't match the ID scanned, but Angelo's facility doesn't have it yet. A rookie never should've been assigned to that section of the prison, and I'll be having a serious conversation with the warden about his tactics."

Motherfucker.

Pinching the bridge of my nose, I ask, "Why wasn't I notified of his escape?"

"You should've been. Someone dropped the ball on that one and you can be rest assured I'll be looking into it."

Getting confirmation that Angelo is free and after me once again has a feeling of stone-cold dread slithering down my spine. The fact I'd been thinking about the past more often lately should've been a clue. On a subconscious level, I somehow knew this was coming. *Maybe it was fate sending me a warning.* Angelo is the type to taunt me with the knowledge that he's out there and can get to me at any time so I'm completely out of my mind before he strikes. It can happen anywhere at any time, and I'll likely never see it coming.

I should hire someone to watch my back.

The idea is sound, and I find myself blurting, "Do you know of any reputable security companies that offer bodyguards? Angelo is the kind of threat that'll come from the shadows when I least expect it and I'd feel safer having someone watching my back."

Krealik says, "I could look into it for you, but I have a better idea. Valik and I are taking some time off, so we'll be in Asphalt Bay for a while and won't need guards with us all the time. We can probably spare someone from our own personal security team."

Shoulders sagging in relief, I say, "That would be great, thank you."

I hear a phone ping in the background and Krealik says, "No problem. My mate texted Valik and he's good with us assigning one of our guards to you.

I've got the perfect candidate in mind. He's ex special forces and has been the head of our security team for years. Dealing with threats is his specialty. He'll keep you safe."

"This means a lot to me. Thank you so much."

"It's no trouble at all. I'll text Teagan and have him head your way now. He's just come off a double shift, so he'll need sleep, but I think you'll feel safer just by having him in the house. Plus, he's a light sleeper thanks to years spent in combat zones and on high alert, so if someone breaks in, he'll be wide awake at the first misplaced sound." *He has a point. I would feel safer with someone else in the house.*

"I should probably mention that him staying with me will likely place a target on his back." The last thing I want is for Teagan to be unprepared for the danger he'll be in and have him get hurt. I'd never forgive myself if another innocent person was killed by Angelo just because he's obsessed with me.

"That's a foregone conclusion Alaric. I'm reading the file on Angelo, so I know the second Teagan enters your house, he'll be on Angelo's radar. Angelo is unpredictable right now because we don't know if he's still operating with the fantasy of the two of you being in a relationship or if he's of the mindset to make you pay for the wrong you committed by testifying against him."

Pinching the bridge of my nose, I tell him, "I have a feeling it's the latter. The package I got is a testament to that fact."

"I'll contact the Asphalt Bay police and have them send someone over to collect the box from you and get your statement. We'll want to have every incident documented in case we need to bring Angelo to trial again. I've got a feeling this is only going to end one way." *That one way being someone, either me or him, or even both of us ends up dead.*

"I'm thinking the same."

"Teagan is on his way and should be at your address in fifteen minutes. The police will probably beat him there."

I'd ask how he got my address, but I already know. He's a councilman so he's got access to a lot of information. Telling Krealik, "Thanks again," I end the call and head to my living room to wait for the officer and Teagan to arrive.

Chapter 4

Getting a phone call from Krealik in the middle of the night an hour after I'd fallen asleep means I'm running on fumes as I maneuver my Harley through the streets of Asphalt Bay. Since Asphalt Bay is a small town, everything is closed up by ten in the evening, so the streets are practically deserted. Which is great for me seeing as I probably shouldn't be driving at all with how tired I am. Deserted streets mean less of a risk for me to get into an accident with someone if my tiredness gets the best of me. My phone's GPS is feeding directions to me through the Bluetooth in my helmet. Beyond the need to go to the store for groceries so the cabin me and the other guards are staying in is fully stocked, I haven't explored the town, so I don't know my way around yet.

Most of my time is split between work and sleep so days off for me are few and far between. I thought I'd finally have some time off now that Krealik and Valik are taking time for themselves, but this new assignment has proven me wrong. Hopefully, I can draw out the person threatening Alaric and end this assignment quickly so I can take a vacation. It's been at least a decade since I took one and I'm in need of some R&R.

Parking my Harley next to the truck in Alaric's driveway, I cut the engine and remove my helmet. Sliding the keys in my pocket, I get off the bike, unstrap the duffel from the back and head for the front door where a tall man with short hair so blonde it's almost white is waiting for me. *This must be Alaric.* He's wearing a black tank top and tan cargo shorts. A large black bandage covering his chest peeks out from the collar of his shirt and I can't help but wonder if he was injured somehow. Alaric has his arms crossed and it makes his muscles bulge. He's ruggedly handsome with icy silver eyes and angular features and I'm suddenly paralyzed by the electric spark of instant attraction that hits me at the sight of him.

Shaking off the feeling, I make my way up the concrete steps. Standing in front of Alaric, I hold out my hand and say, "Hi, I'm Teagan."

Alaric smiles slightly and says with a hint of a Russian accent, "Alaric. It's nice to meet you Teagan though I wish it was under different circumstances. Come on in."

Alaric steps back and I walk into the house, brushing past him. As I do, his scent of ginger, marshmallow, and raspberry hits me in the face making my cock stand up and take notice. The sudden surge of arousal and my animal half roaring *mine* in my head shocks me to the core. *Well, this is an interesting development.*

I don't realize I've voiced the thought aloud until Alaric asks, "What's an interesting development," as he closes the front door and locks it.

Grinning at him, I say, "We're mates."

Alaric's eyes widen and the scent of fear hits my nose as he backs away from me so quickly he bumps into the entry table, knocking a bowl to the floor where it shatters. Alaric grips his short hair and tugs on it. His breathing is coming fast with his rising panic, and he shakes his head, whispering to himself, "This can't be happening. It can't. It just can't." Knowing he's scared and panicking doesn't stop the pain that stabs my heart as his words reach my ears. When I envisioned meeting my mate, this is not how I thought it would go.

Alaric disappears up the stairs in a blur and I hear the sound of a door slamming. Unsure if I should go after him or give him space, I stay where I'm at. *Maybe he'll come back when he's calmed down.* Sighing, I scrub my hands over my face and head for the living room deciding to give him space for now. Dropping my duffel bag on the floor, I remove the backpack I'm wearing and put it next to the duffel. Kicking off my boots, I tuck them out of the way under the coffee table and lay on the couch. Thank gods Alaric's couch is one of those long sectionals otherwise I wouldn't fit thanks to my height.

As soon as my head hits the cushion, a yawn overtakes me. *Fuck, I'm tired.* Linking my hands behind my head, I close my eyes and pray for sleep to take me even though I have a feeling I won't be getting any tonight. My thoughts are swirling too much for it. It doesn't help that when I'm woken prematurely from sleep it takes forever to get back there. Sometimes I never manage it. I'm trying not to take Alaric's actions as a clear sign of rejection, but it's hard.

After an hour of laying here no closer to sleep, I hear Alaric's footsteps on the stairs, but I don't move to get up. I don't want to spook him and cause a repeat performance of earlier. The couch cushion by my head dips as Alaric sits down. Still, I keep my eyes closed, waiting for what he'll do. Alaric's fingers drift through my hair and I open my eyes to find him watching me. "I'm sorry for earlier."

"It's okay."

Alaric shakes his head. "It's not, but I'd like to explain myself."

Nodding, I scoot up until my head is in his lap so he can keep running his fingers through my hair and say, "I'm listening."

"I don't know how much of my situation Krealik divulged to you."

"Not much. He just said you needed protection from someone who'd escaped from a council jail."

Alaric sighs. "Fifty years ago, Angelo was stalking me. In his head, we were in a relationship, and he killed every person I had a one-night stand with because he saw them as a threat to that relationship. I felt guilty because if I hadn't slept with them, they'd still be alive. Despite the fact he was caught and sent to jail, I couldn't stop wondering what would've happened had I met my beloved while he was still after me. It was my worst fear and still is to this day."

Understanding dawns and I state the obvious. "You're terrified something will happen to me now that he's escaped custody and is coming after you again."

"Yes. The thought that you'd become his target when he finds out about you sent me into a panic. We're fated and losing you would kill me."

Reaching up, I grip the back of his head and pull him down so he's looking directly into my eyes. "Listen to me. You don't have to worry. I can handle myself. I spent twenty years in the Army before I retired. I was Delta Force, did three tours in Afghanistan and went on missions in countries we weren't even supposed to be in. I've seen what hell looks like, been shot at, stabbed, nearly bombed and still came out on top. I've been a council guardsman for the last ten years and I train with other guards three sometimes four times a week. Whatever Angelo has planned, has nothing on me and the shit I can do."

Pointing to my bags, I wink at him, "I even brought my special bag of tricks."

Alaric laughs and says, "I look forward to seeing what you've brought. While it might be silly, I can't help but hope you won't have to use any of it."

Stroking his cheek with my thumb, I shake my head. "It's not silly to have hope. Anything can happen. Angelo could get hit by a bus crossing the street tomorrow and we wouldn't know until we saw it on the news."

Alaric snorts. "I've lived long enough to know nothing is ever that easy. Doesn't matter how much we wish it was. It sounds harsh but I'd love for Angelo to get hit by a bus tomorrow. At least then I'd finally have peace of mind knowing there's no chance he'll ever come back to threaten me again."

Looking into his eyes, I tell him seriously, "He'll have to go through me first. I won't let him get to you. I swear it."

Alaric sighs and nods. "I know you will, but I hope you won't do it at the expense of your own safety. I don't want to lose you after only just finding you."

"You won't lose me. I'll take every step to keep myself safe while making that prick regret coming after you again."

A grin stretches across Alaric's face, showing off his fangs. "You sound more bloodthirsty than I am. Are you sure you're not part vampire?"

The teasing tone to his voice makes me laugh but it turns into a yawn when I say, "I'm sure."

Alaric pats my shoulder and says, "Come on, *vozlyublennyy,* let's go to bed. You're exhausted and need your rest."

Standing, I let him take my hand and lead me up the stairs. We pass open doorways revealing empty rooms until we reach the end of the hall. I'll get him to give me a tour of the house tomorrow. I'm too tired to take in all the details and plan for security upgrades. Alaric opens the double-oak doors to reveal a large master bedroom. The blue silk sheets on his king size bed are calling my name. Leaving Alaric to close the bedroom doors, I head for the side of the bed that doesn't have Alaric's things on the nightstand.

Removing my keys, wallet, and phone from my pockets, I put them on the nightstand and crawl into bed. Alaric crawls in beside me and says, "You know, you don't have to sleep in your jeans. If you need something else to wear, I can go downstairs and get your bags, or you can borrow something of mine."

"I grabbed my go-bag instead of taking the time to pack a bunch of clothes when security tech and weapons seemed more important, so I only have one other set of clothes. Cargo pants are more comfortable than jeans but if you've got an extra pair of athletic shorts, I'll take them. We can go by my place tomorrow and I can grab the rest of my stuff and bring it here. That's if you don't mind me moving in with you."

Alaric grins at me and says, "I'd love nothing more than for you to move in and I mean permanently, not just for the duration of your bodyguard duties. In case you were wondering."

Chuckling, I shake my head. "I wasn't but thanks for clarifying."

Alaric uses his vampire speed to grab me a pair of shorts and I change into them without leaving the bed. When I kick my jeans onto the floor, Alaric laughs. "I see you're a man of many talents."

Yawning, I pull him closer so I can snuggle with him and say, "When I'm one-hundred-percent rested, I'll show you just how talented I can be."

The innuendo in that statement doesn't go unnoticed and Alaric purrs, "Looking forward to it, now get some sleep *vozlyublennyy*."

Nodding, I close my eyes and bury my nose in his neck. His scent helps clear my mind of racing thoughts and it doesn't take long for sleep to claim me.

Chapter 5

I'm awake before Teagan but instead of getting up to start my day, I'm watching him sleep. His mouth is slightly open and gentle snores escape him. His military short black hair is sticking up in all directions and the black t-shirt he's wearing has ridden up to mid-back showing off the bottom part of an impressive military themed tattoo. To normal eyes, no one would notice the scarring the ink hides, but I see it. There are jagged lines from a knife or shrapnel and bullet wounds. I want to explore the rest of his ink and get the story behind every scar if he'll tell me. I wish I'd kissed him last night, but I'll rectify that as soon as he wakes up.

As I'm watching him, a grin stretches across his face though his eyes are still closed. "I can feel your eyes on me, creeper." The teasing tone of his voice makes me smile.

"What can I say, you're damn fine to look at, *vozlyublennyy*. It's not every day I wake up with a sexy man in my bed, snoring in my ear."

His bright green eyes fly open, and he growls. "I do not snore."

Barking out a laugh, I tap his nose with my finger which he gnashes his teeth at, like he's going to bite me. "Oh yes you do. It's not chainsaw snoring or freight train snoring. It's cute little huffs."

Teagan's eyes narrow and he rolls until he's straddling me. "I'm a badass and badasses aren't cute."

Walking my fingers up his muscled chest, I bop his nose again and tease, "Who's a cutie? You are. Yes, you are."

Teagan laughs. "Okay, baby talk is going a bit too far there, *hekili*."

Chuckling, I shrug and tell him, "Maybe but the look on your face was worth it. Now, what's on the agenda for this morning?"

Teagan leans forward and says huskily, "Well first, I'd like a kiss then I want breakfast and a tour of the house so I can get an idea of what I want to do for extra security measures. After that, we'll go get my stuff and then do whatever we want for the rest of the day."

Happy to oblige his request, I close the distance between us and press my lips to his. Nipping his bottom lip with my fang causes a bead of blood to well up and I swipe my tongue across it, moaning at the taste. It makes me want more. Teagan opens for me, and I deepen the kiss, cradling his head to keep him where I want him. One of Teagan's hands slides down the back of my tank-top through the neck hole while his other hand rests on my cheek. Arousal surges through me and I move my hands to Teagan's hips so I can grind my hard cock against his.

Teagan moans into my mouth and the hand on my cheek moves into my hair. His growl of frustration when he realizes it's too short to grip makes me laugh. Teagan pulls away to catch his breath and I kiss my way down his jaw to his neck. My fangs tingle with the urge to bite and begin the bonding process between us. Before I can ask his permission to do so, Teagan says, "Go ahead, *hekili,* take what you need."

Licking his neck, I sink my fangs into his jugular vein and drink. Teagan's breath starts to come in pants, and he rocks his hips, seeking friction. Slipping my hand into his shorts, I grip his cock and stroke it. Between my hand and the pleasure caused by my bite, it doesn't take long for Teagan to come. The scent of which is enough to send me over the edge myself. Having taken enough blood, I pull back and lick the wound to seal it. Leaning back, I take in the blissed-out expression on Teagan's face. Already, I look forward to putting that look on his face again. While I'd love to finish bonding with him right now, we've got shit to do so it'll have to wait until later.

Looking at the mess we've made, I grin at Teagan and say, "Let's get cleaned up and then I'll fix us breakfast."

Teagan moves off my lap and heads for the bathroom, stripping off his clothes as he goes. His body is a work of art and I wish we had the time for me to explore every inch of him. *Later, Alaric.* Climbing off the bed, I strip and follow Teagan into the bathroom. He's already got the water running for the shower and is waiting for it to heat. When he sees me approaching, he closes the distance between us and places his hand on my chest. "What happened here?"

Looking down, I see he's talking about the bandage covering my tattoo. Vic said it was to keep any dirt or bacteria from getting into it until it had healed. I was supposed to remove the bandage when I got home but in the chaos of last night, I forgot about it. Pulling the bandage off, I let him see the design. "I got a tattoo yesterday. With everything that happened last night, I forgot to take the bandage off."

Teagan's eyes widen when he sees the design and he traces part of it with his fingertip. "What made you choose this?"

Shrugging, I tell him, "I can't explain it. It just called to me. Why? Is something wrong with it?"

Teagan shakes his head and smiles. "It reminds me of me. I'm a grizzly bear shifter and I was born in a small town near the Colorado Rockies. The trees and mountains looked a lot like this."

Chuckling, I say, "I guess fate had a hand in my decision."

"Maybe she did. It wouldn't surprise me. Fate does work in mysterious ways."

Stepping into the shower, I tug him in behind me so we can get cleaned up. The stall is cramped with the two of us in here, but we manage to finish with only a couple accidental elbow strikes. As we're drying off, Teagan asks, "Do you like how this bathroom looks?"

I shake my head. "Not really. Everything in here is white on white and as you surely noticed, the shower is small. So is the bathtub. By master bathroom standards it's sorely lacking."

"So, you wouldn't be opposed to remodeling?"

The thought of us making this house into a home together fills me with warmth. "Not at all, *vozlyublennyy.* If you don't like something, we'll change it. I want this to be our home, so your input matters. I've been wanting to remodel since my roommates moved out and I had the title to the house transferred into just my name and not all of ours. Now we can do it together, so everything suits us both."

Teagan nods and flashes a grin at me. "I like the sound of that."

His stomach growls suddenly and I laugh. "I think that's my cue to feed you."

Teagan shrugs and wraps the towel around his hips. Following him out of the bathroom, I head for my dresser where I pull out a pair of cargo shorts and a Rolling Stones t-shirt. Once dressed, I head downstairs. Teagan is in the living room pulling on a pair of cargo pants when I pass him on my way into the kitchen. I'd have stopped to watch but that would lead to a repeat of earlier and I think Teagan's stomach would stage a mutiny if it had to wait any longer to be satiated. *And I can't believe I'm talking about his stomach like it's a person.*

Shaking my head at my dumbass thoughts, I search the fridge for something to make. I need to go shopping and after making a fancy omelet yesterday, my options are limited. Grabbing bacon and the last of the eggs, I close the fridge and put everything on the counter while I get a pot of coffee brewing. I completely forgot to set it up last night so it would brew automatically. Oops.

Teagan comes into the kitchen and asks, "Need help with anything?"

Pressing the button to start the coffee brewing, I shake my head. "Nope, I've got it. You just sit your gorgeous ass down and let me cook for you."

Teagan grins and teases, "Your wish is my command Mr. Bossy-pants."

Teasing right back, I tell him, "And don't you forget it."

Teagan barks out a laugh and gives me a quick kiss before he pours himself a cup of coffee from the still-brewing pot and goes to sit at the island. Grabbing a pan, I get to work fixing breakfast.

Chapter 6

After breakfast, I help Alaric clean up before he leads me through the house showing me the laundry room, backyard, and basement music studio before we head upstairs. "As you saw last night, there are only three bedrooms. I'd love to add a couple more when we remodel. I've always wanted a big family. In the coven I grew up in, there weren't many kids to play with and my parents didn't have any more after me."

Seeing the sad look on his face, I ask, "Why's that?"

"Mom had fertility issues. She had three miscarriages before me and six more after. It took a toll on her and my dad, so they quit trying. Adoption wasn't really a thing back then, so I was all they had, and they doted on me."

Unable to resist the urge to comfort him, I rub my hand across his back. "I take it by your use of past tense, they aren't around anymore?"

Alaric shakes his head. "They died during World War I when a bomb was dropped on the coven house. I was in Australia at the time."

"I'm sorry to hear that. My parents are gone too. A wildfire wiped out my entire sleuth. Luckily, my two younger sisters were away at college at the time, so I still have them."

Alaric smiles at me and says, "I'm glad you have them."

"They're great and they're moving here. I can't wait for you to meet them."

Alaric kisses me softly, eyes alight with happiness. "I'm looking forward to it. I'll have to introduce you to my bandmates sometime soon. They're basically my family now."

Raising an eyebrow at him, I question, "Bandmates?"

Alaric grins. "You're looking at the drummer for The Dead Tuesdays. We have a permanent contract with the Blue Moon club in Venetian Hills playing three nights a week."

Well shit. My mate's a Rockstar. Grinning widely, I tease, "You just made me want to act out every hot rockstar fantasy I've ever had."

Alaric winks at me. "I'll help you fulfill all your fantasies anytime you want, *vozlyublennyy.*"

Arousal surges through me and I shiver then a thought occurs and my eyes narrow as I let them roam over Alaric's sexy body and imagine him wearing typical rocker garb while sitting behind a drum kit. "I'll have to beat the groupies off you with a stick."

Alaric barks out a laugh and moves into my space until he's pressed against me. "None of them will ever compare to you, *vozlyublennyy.*"

Growling, "Damn right they won't," I take his lips in a fiery hot kiss that makes me want to say screw it and take him to bed instead of doing what needs to be done. When we pull apart, Alaric's icy silver eyes have darkened with lust. He licks his lips and says, "Tour's over, *vozlyublennyy.* Let's go get your stuff before I drag you into our room and refuse to let you leave until we're both thoroughly claimed."

Licking my lips, I tell him, "*Helkini,* you talk like that's some kind of threat when I'd be more than willing to take you up on what you're offering."

Alaric's gaze drifts down to the hard-on tenting the front of my cargo pants and chuckles. "I can see that, but we both know you'd never forgive yourself if something were to happen because we put off getting the security stuff set up."

Knowing he's right, I take his hand and say, "Then let's go. The sooner we get my shit, the sooner we can come back, get security set up, and move on to the fun stuff."

Alaric squeezes my hand and leads me downstairs. Before we exit the house, he looks out the window checking for anyone or anything suspicious. I know Angelo won't make it that easy unless he's of a mind to taunt Alaric with seeing him. Seemingly satisfied that nothing is amiss, Alaric opens the front door and curses. Looking over his shoulder, I see a black box tied with red ribbon on the porch. Alaric uses the hold he still has on my hand to pull me out onto the porch with him. After he makes sure the door is locked he leads me to his truck completely ignoring the box.

I can tell by the tense set of his shoulders and the darkening of his mood that the box's arrival isn't a good thing. Once we're inside his truck, Alaric hits the door locks then pulls out his phone and a business card and dials the number on it. When the person on the other end of the phone picks up, Alaric says, "Hello Detective Davis, this is Alaric Glazkov, I found another box on my doorstep this morning. I left it where it is and didn't touch or open it."

Alaric starts the truck's engine, and his call connects to it just as Detective Davis says, "I'll send a crime scene tech over to take pictures and collect the box."

Alaric seems relieved when he tells the Detective, "Thank you, I won't be home when the tech arrives, so if you need anything else from me, call."

Detective Davis says, "I don't think I'll need anything else but if I do, I'll call," and hangs up.

Alaric sighs and tucks the phone and business card back into his pocket. Reaching out, I put my hand on his bicep and squeeze it gently. "I take it the box is from Angelo?"

He nods. "Yeah. The first one came yesterday and is what sparked me to call Krealik. When I opened it, Angelo was the first to come to mind but I told myself it had to be someone else because Angelo was in prison."

"And then you found out that he wasn't in prison anymore."

"Right. Krealik said he's been out for two weeks. It gave him plenty of time to find me and follow my every move before giving me the first box. I don't know how he managed to get into a locked truck, but after going through this once before, I know not to underestimate him."

Alaric puts the truck in gear and backs out of the driveway. I don't ask how he knows to go to pack lands because it's the obvious choice. It's not like there's anywhere else nearby safe enough for the councilmen to stay without needing guards all the time. I'm glad Krealik's mate is a demon capable of opening portals to wherever we need to go otherwise I'd have to look at retiring from the council guard.

With Alaric being in a band and performing at the same place multiple nights a week, he can't travel with me and be gone for days when I need to accompany the councilmen somewhere. With a portal, if he wants to come with me, we can make sure he gets to his performances on time, or I can use one to come home every night. It would mean switching from night shift to days and being on call for emergencies but I'm willing to make the change. We may have just met, but I already know I'd do anything for him.

When we arrive at pack lands, I give Alaric directions to the cabin I've been staying at with the other guards. It's a small two-bedroom cottage so we've had to share rooms whenever we're here. I've got a room to myself since Matt is off right now. Fate has timed things just right with me meeting Alaric. Since Krealik and Valik are taking time off and sticking to Asphalt Bay they'll only need two guards max which means I can take the time I'll need to bond with Alaric while also dealing with the situation he's in. *I can't wait to get him alone.*

Alaric asks teasingly, "What's that grin for?"

Winking at him, I say, "Thinking about getting you alone later."

He barks out a laugh and parks in front of the cabin beside the bulletproof SUV we drive Krealik and Valik around in. The door of the cabin opens and Zach steps out, followed by James. Both of them fold their arms and look at the truck with scowls on their faces. The truck's windshield being tinted makes it hard to see who's inside, so I'm not surprised they're wary of our arrival. Hopping out of the truck, I grin and shout, "You two assholes shouldn't glare so much. It makes you look constipated."

Alaric -having jumped out of the truck at the same time I did- doubles over with laughter and it makes me smile wider. I love knowing I can bring him some happiness in spite of the shit he's going through right now. Zach and Jeff both roll their eyes and give me back slapping bro hugs when I step up onto the porch. Zach looks over my shoulder at Alaric and asks, "Who's this?"

Reaching behind me, I take Alaric's hand and pull him up so he's standing at my side. "This is Alaric, my mate."

Zach grins widely. "Congratulations man." Jeff's brows are furrowed in confusion, and he tilts his head to the side. "I thought you were on some new assignment for Krealik."

"I am. Alaric is the assignment. I realized he's my mate when I showed up on his doorstep last night."

Jeff smiles then and pats me on the back. "Well, congratulations are in order then. Nothing compares to the love of a mate. I'm happy for you my friend."

Zach reaches out and takes Jeff's hand, kissing the back of it. Even after ten years, the fact these two are mates still boggles my mind. You'd think after so long, I'd get used to seeing them show affection for one another but it's still just as adorable now as it was when they met. I remember when all of us were first assigned together as a team. Council guards are trained in classes of twenty-five and rotate between different instructors. The four of us were in separate classes so when we were put together Zach and Jeff realized they were mates. Watching them fall in love was an experience and the fact they've been conquering the demands and dangers of the job together is amazing.

Jeff turns to Alaric and says while pointing at me with his thumb, "I don't know where this one's manners are but I'm Jeff and this is Zach. It's lovely to meet you."

Alaric chuckles. "It's nice to meet you too."

Zach gestures to the door with a nod of his head and says, "Come on inside. We've got coffee and donuts."

Following them inside, I tell Zach, "We've already eaten but thanks for the offer. We're just here to get my stuff."

Zach teases, "Aw you're moving out. Look hon, our little bird is leaving the nest."

Jeff wipes away a fake tear and sniffles, "It's wonderful dear."

Rolling my eyes at their antics, I lean over and whisper to Alaric, "Come on, let's get away from the weirdos."

Zach gasps in mock outrage. "Hey, I resent that remark."

Laughing, I take Alaric's hand and lead him down the hall to my room. Matt's stuff is still on his side of the room because this is where we stay whenever Krealik and Valik are home. The twin size beds we sleep on had to be custom made because a normal twin size was nowhere near long enough for our height. Matt uses the dresser while I have the closet. Zach comes in behind us and hands me a box of trash bags.

"Figured you might need these to put your stuff in."

Taking the box from him, I thank him and pull a bag from the box. I don't have a ton of stuff, just clothes, some knickknacks, DVDs, and a few books. Almost all of it will fit in the duffle bag I have at the top of the closet, but the trash bag will work for the rest. When Krealik and Valik decided to make Asphalt Bay their permanent residence, I sold my house and put everything inside it into one of those pod storage containers. The container is being housed at a facility until I decide to have it brought here. There wasn't a need for it while living in the cabin with the rest of the guys but now that I'll be moving in with Alaric, I'll have the container delivered to the house either before or after we remodel.

Alaric takes the trash bag from me and says, "Tell me where to start."

Pointing to my side of the room I tell him, "Everything over here and in the closet is mine. The stuff over there and in the dresser belongs to Matt. He's on vacation right now since he met his mate."

Alaric kisses my cheek and walks over to my nightstand and begins to empty it. Leaving him to it, I head over to the closet and grab my duffle bag from the top shelf. Opening it up, I grab my shoebox of sex toys off the same shelf and put it in the bag first. I haven't used them in forever because it'd be awkward while sharing a room with someone, but I figure Alaric and I can have some fun with them. After adding the small stack of books I've got up there along with my DVDs, I start taking my clothes off the hangers and roll them up as I go so I can fit more in the bag than I would if I just folded them.

The closet isn't one where you can walk in, but it's packed with clothes from wall to wall. When the duffle bag is full, I zip it up and step back so Alaric can start tucking the rest of my clothes inside the trash bag he's been filling. All in all, it takes us about twenty minutes to pack up everything I've got. Which would be sad if I didn't have a storage container with everything from my house in it. Originally, I bought my house with the plan to share it with my mate when I found that person but sometimes plans have to change. I'm looking forward to making Alaric's house something we both love.

I put the duffle strap over my shoulder as Alaric finishes tying shut the trash bag that's stuffed to the brim. He hefts the bag onto his shoulder and looks at me with a smile on his face. "Ready to go, *vozlyublennyy*."

Nodding my head, I beam at him. "Let's blow this popsicle stand, *helkini*."

Leaving the room, we head out. Zach and Jeff are still in the kitchen, so we say our goodbyes as we pass them. Once outside, we put my bags in the backseat and wave at Zach and Jeff who shout from the porch as I get ready to climb into the truck. "You come back to visit anytime," as if I'm moving out of state instead of fifteen minutes down the road.

Shaking my head at their antics, I climb into the truck and say, "Take me home, *helkini.*"

Chapter 7

I break the speed limit all the way home. With arousal surging through me at the prospect of finally claiming what's mine, I feel like my dick is the one doing the driving, not me. While I'm still worried, I can't let the fear of what Angelo will do keep me from my forever. The fact that I'll die with him if we're fully claimed is a comfort. Sure, it would suck to have our lives cut short but at least we'll be together and this thing with Angelo will be over. That and the knowledge Teagan can take care of himself is the reason I have the courage to throw caution to the wind and take what I want.

The tires squeal as I brake hard pulling into the driveway. Teagan is laughing as I throw the truck in park. Hopping out, I race for the front door studiously ignoring the spot where the box was. Teagan's footsteps sound behind me as he runs to catch up with me. Once we're through the door, we're on each other, lips meeting with a ferocity I've never experienced before. Teagan's bag hits the floor with a thud. I didn't even realize he'd grabbed it. His hands tug at my shirt and I back away from him long enough to let him pull it over my head. Fisting his t-shirt, I rip it down the middle letting the scraps fall from his arms. Teagan looks at the ruined fabric and laughs. His voice is teasing when he says, "I would've taken it off. You didn't have to rip it."

Shrugging, I grin at him, "Where's the fun in that?"

Teagan's grin turns feral, and he grabs my shorts, ripping them down the middle in similar fashion to what I did with his shirt. As my shorts fall away in scraps, Teagan's gaze roves over my naked body. "You're right, this is way more fun."

Laughing, I kick off my shoes and socks before I pull him to me by his belt so I can take his lips in a kiss again. Keeping hold of the belt, I walk us toward the stairs so we can take this to the bedroom. We bump into the wall knocking pictures and artwork off as we climb. I trip on the last stair and fall on my ass pulling Teagan down on top of me. Teagan's hands frame my face, and he asks, "Are you okay?"

Chuckling, I nod at him and say, "I'm good." Teagan gets to his feet and holds out his hand. Taking it, I let him pull me up then use the hold to drag him down the hall to the bedroom where I push him onto the bed. He's still wearing his cargo pants and boots and it's sexy as hell. All he needs is a fake badge and a SWAT hat and it'd be like he walked right out of my favorite cop porno. *Something to keep in mind for another time.* We could have so much fun playing cops and robbers the naughty version.

Teagan says, "I'd love to know what put that look on your face."

Grinning at him, I say, "I was thinking about a cops and robbers naughty roleplay. You've got more of these cargo pants right?" As the question leaves my lips, I rub my hands over his thighs.

Teagan chuckles. "You know I do, *helkini.*"

Unbuckling his belt, I pull it through the loops and toss it on the floor. Teagan kicks off his boots and socks and reaches for the button on his pants. Smacking his hands away, I say, "Let me," and take over. When I have his pants undone, Teagan lifts his hips so I can pull them off. His hard cock slaps against his belly and I grin. "Commando huh? I like it."

Tossing his pants on the floor, I climb onto his lap. Teagan's hands slide up my legs to my ass where he pulls me against him, so our hard cocks are pressed together. Using the hold he has on me to keep me in place, Teagan scoots us up the bed. Leaning over, I grab the lube from the nightstand and hand it to him. Before Teagan can say anything about it, I press my lips to his. I don't usually bottom because it's not my preference but for Teagan, I want to. More than anything.

Teagan puts the lube down so it's within reach leaving his hands free to explore. Which he takes full advantage of, letting those hands move over my body in gentle explorative motions that only serve to tease me. His lips move from mine to travel down my jaw and neck. When he gets to my fully healed tattoo, he traces every line with his tongue, driving me out of my mind with need. Just as I'm about to start begging for him to get a move on, he opens the lube and pours some onto his fingers.

When he starts circling my hole with a fingertip, I almost tense. It takes me telling myself to relax in order to allow his finger entry. It's been a very, very, long time since I bottomed for anyone. So long in fact, I'm practically a born-again virgin. The thought makes me snort and has Teagan raising an eyebrow at me. "It's been a while since I bottomed."

Teagan nods and winks at me. "I'll be gentle."

Chuckling, I lean forward and press my lips to his, using our kiss to distract me from what he's doing with his fingers. After a few minutes, he ends the kiss, removes his fingers, and asks, "Ready?"

Nodding my head, I guide his cock to my hole and slowly sink down onto him. He's huge, bigger than anyone I recall ever having before. Add in the time it's been since I've done this and I'm feeling the burn of being stretched to my limits despite the prep Teagan put in. By the time I've taken all of him, sweat is pouring off me and my breath is coming in pants. I'm also pretty sure my face is red as fuck from the exertion. Teagan looks up at me with concern and asks, "Are you okay?"

Giving him a smile, I say, "I'm fine, I just need a minute."

"Take your time. I'm not going anywhere," he tells me with a teasing tone and a wag of his eyebrows.

Snorting a laugh, I shake my head at him before giving my hips an experimental wiggle. Feeling okay, I raise myself up before lowering again setting a slow steady rhythm. With a growl, Teagan grips my hips to hold me in place before he rolls us so he's on top. Grinning like a loon at the expression on his face, I tease, "Was I not moving fast enough for you?"

His response is to glare at me before a feral grin crosses his face and he starts to move. All I can do is hang on for the ride and moan like a porn star because that's apparently a thing I do now. When he begins to peg my prostate on every thrust, I get closer and closer to the edge. Wrapping my arms around

Teagan, I pull him down to me, taking note of the way his eyes change to the black ones of his animal half. Knowing what's coming, I tilt my head to the side, exposing my neck. Teagan's gaze zeroes in on it and a possessively growled, "Mine," is all the warning I get before he strikes, sinking his teeth into my neck and claiming me as his. The bite rips my orgasm from me, and I paint both our chests with it.

Teagan removes his teeth and licks the wound to seal it before gently easing out of me and collapsing at my side. Putting my hand on his shoulder, I push him onto his back and lean over him. "Now, it's my turn."

Teagan holds out his arms and says, "Have at me, *helkini*."

Purring at him, I swipe a fingertip down his chest and say huskily, "Oh I plan to, *vozlyublennyy*."

Teagan
Chapter 8

I wake to the sound of glass breaking followed by a whooshing sound. Easing out from under Alaric who fell asleep on top of me after we claimed each other, I grab the gun I left on the nightstand and make my way downstairs. I'm only halfway there when I see the orange flames licking up the curtains and engulfing the furniture in the living room. *Motherfucker.* Someone threw a Molotov cocktail through the window. Turning on my heels, I run back up the stairs and head straight for Alaric. Shaking him awake, I say, "The living room is on fire, we've got to get out of here."

Alaric stares at me wide-eyed before leaping from bed and heading for the closet. He tosses me some clothes that I quickly put on and hands me my bag of toys we stashed in there after we came up for air to venture into the kitchen for food last night. Seeing the bag reminds me of my original plans for today and I could kick myself for letting my cock and my instincts get in the way of my job. Instead of claiming Alaric when we got back, I should've put up security cameras and set some traps so we could catch Angelo before he got near the house. Did I do that? Nooo, because I let my cock overrule my head. *Idiot.*

With no time to continue to berate myself, I take a now-dressed Alaric's hand and lead him to the bedroom window. Opening it up, I take a quick look around knowing we'll have to be on our guard as soon as we go out. Not seeing anything, I say, "Let's go," and jump out the window first. Being a paranormal with stronger bones and healing abilities, a two-story drop isn't going to do anything to me or Alaric. Keeping my gun trained on our surroundings, I wait for Alaric to join me and tell him, "Stay behind me. We're going to make our way around the front of the house to your truck."

Alaric curses. "Shit, I don't have the keys."

"That's okay. I can hotwire it." I just hope neither of our vehicles have been tampered with. Otherwise, we'll be sitting ducks if Angelo decides to make another move tonight. I have a feeling we're seeing his end game here. The fire was just a way to smoke us out and now is when the real fight will begin. He should've been waiting for us here in the back. From a tactical standpoint, picking us off as we exited the house through the window would've been Angelo's best shot to get us both. Though if Angelo hasn't spent any time in the military, he might not know that. Or he could know we'd probably head straight for the vehicles and that's where he'll have set up his trap.

Keeping a tight grip on Alaric's hand that borders on bruising, I lead him stealthily around the side of the house, keeping close to it so we remain in the shadows. Peeking around the corner, I see both our vehicles are sitting a little lower to the ground than they should be meaning Angelo must've slashed the tires. *Damn it.* Alaric squeezes my hand but instead of voicing his question he uses our mind link.

What's wrong?

We need a new escape route. The tires on the vehicles have been slashed.

What if we go back and cross the neighbor's yard until we're far enough away that we can make a break for the police station and let them know what's happening.

Movement to our right draws my attention and I duck back before I'm seen by the man who is pacing back and forth in front of our house shouting "Come out come out wherever you are." The orange glow of the flames casts him in a glow making it evident the man hasn't seen a shower in days. The clothes he's wearing are torn in places, covered in dirt and there's twigs and leaves in his hair and unkempt beard like he's been sleeping outside. You'd think someone who managed to escape council custody and hunt down the person they're obsessed with would have some resources. Like a place to stay, cash, and clean clothes but apparently not. Either he had limited funds and means or he stole everything he's needed to intimidate Alaric, like the gifts and the stuff for the Molotov cocktail.

Sirens in the distance alert me to the fact someone must've called in the fire which means shit is about to go sideways. Angelo will either run and try again another time or this whole thing will result in a standoff between him and first responders. The AK-47 he pulls out from under the long trench coat he's wearing settles the debate. *Stand-off.* With a gun like that and enough bullets, he can take out every single first responder that shows up here until he gets what he's after. *Alaric.* Not willing to let that happen, I turn to Alaric. Cradling his face between my hands, I peck a kiss to his lips and say, "I'm going to distract him, you run through the neighbor's yard and see if you can cut off the first responders before they get too close, and he starts shooting."

Alaric shakes his head and whispers furiously, "No way. I'm not leaving you."

"I can handle myself, remember? Go."

"No. We're in this together. Let's take him out before it's too late."

Seeing the determined look on his face, I know I won't win this battle. "Fine. You circle around the other side of the house. I'll distract him and you come up behind him to subdue him."

"He'll shoot you on sight. I'll distract him, you subdue."

Raising an eyebrow at him, I question, "And how do you know he won't shoot you?"

Alaric shrugs. "I don't. It's a risk I'm willing to take though. Just like you are."

Growling, I run my fingers through my hair and tell him, "I hate this plan."

He squeezes my bicep and says, "I know but I think I'm the better choice. If I can talk to him and keep him distracted, you'll have a chance to subdue him."

Knowing he's right, I rub a hand over my face and say, "Fine, but you're not going out there unarmed so take this. I'd give you a gun, but he might shoot you if he sees it and I don't want you getting hurt."

Opening my bag of toys, I pull out a special grenade and hand it to him. "If you think he's about to shoot, pull the pin on this and throw it at his feet."

Alaric takes the grenade with furrowed brows. "Won't I be in the blast zone if I do that?"

I shake my head. "This isn't that kind of grenade. This one will hit him with sixty thousand volts of electricity. It's enough force to take down a rogue vampire that's succumbed to bloodlust, so it'll take his ass out without a problem. I got it from a friend who used to work as a council assassin before he became a hitman for hire. He's retired now but still develops this kind of shit for fun."

Alaric chuckles. "You'll have to tell me more about this guy when we're not about to be in the fight of our lives."

Winking at him, I say, "You got it. I'll take the rest of these with me. If I can't get close enough to subdue him by hand, I'll throw a taser grenade at him and do it that way."

Alaric nods and touches my cheek. "Be safe."

"Ditto." Kissing him one more time, I watch with bated breath and a shit-ton of worry as he steps out of the shadows and heads for Angelo. As soon as Angelo says, "There you are," I jog toward the back of the house. *Please be okay, helkini.*

Chapter 9

I can't believe I'm offering myself up as bait. If it means keeping Teagan out of harm's way and stopping Angelo once and for all, I'd do it every day of the week. I can feel the heat from the flames engulfing the house as I walk towards Angelo. It's so hot and stifling, I feel like I'm about to suffocate. It pisses me off that he set our house on fire. I was looking forward to remodeling the place with Teagan. Now, we'll probably have to tear the whole place down and start over or have my friend Altair magically recreate it as it was before the fire. With Angelo having a gun and needing to protect the first responders, there'll be no saving the house from the flames.

Angelo's attention has been focused solely on me since I stepped out of the shadows of the house, and I need to keep it that way. I know Teagan can handle himself, but it doesn't stop me from worrying about him every second he's out of my sight. If I didn't know Angelo's voice thanks to the trial and all the times I spoke to him before things went too far, I wouldn't even recognize him.

The man used to be clean shaven and baby-faced. The makeup he wore accentuated his model like features and made him look a little bit older than his face suggested. His clothes were always neatly pressed and designed to entice, and his hair was perfectly coiffed into frosted tip spikes at the front. All of that has changed. Gone is the man he used to be and in front of me stands a wild-eyed crazed man who looks like he hasn't seen a shower in weeks and just rolled out of the forest.

Angelo looks me over and says with a manic smile, "It's good to see you again."

Folding my arms, I take care to make sure the grenade isn't seen and tell him, "I wish I could say the same. I'd hoped to never see you again."

Angelo frowns and his eyes light with rage as Teagan's voice booms through our mind link.

Don't provoke him unnecessarily. Are you trying to get yourself shot?

I have to fight not to wince at the volume of his voice in my head.

Sorry. I yell when I'm feeling panicky.

It's okay, I should've thought about how he'd react to my words before speaking.

Angelo's voice draws my attention from the conversation with Teagan. "You know, I thought about how our reunion would go. For fifty years, it was my only comfort. I thought about how when I managed to escape, I'd find you and make you see how much your betrayal hurt me. We had something special, and you threw it away. Threw me away. Like trash. I'm not trash." *Jesus, he's just as delusional now as he was back then.*

As he speaks, Angelo starts waving the gun around with his finger on the trigger, and the threat of being shot ratchets up a little higher. Enough to make me worry. The sirens don't sound like they're getting closer anymore, so Teagan must've stopped them from coming closer before doubling back to get behind Angelo. Angelo's tirade suddenly stops, and his eyes narrow on me. "Wait a minute...where's the other one?"

Playing the fool, I tilt my head to the side and ask, "Who?"

Angelo growls and shakes the gun at me. "Don't patronize me. You know what I'm talking about. The interloper who stole you from me. Where...is...he?" Each word of his question is punctuated by a thrust of the weapon, and I know I'll be in deep shit if I don't come up with something to tell him.

The smoke from the fire has my eyes starting to water which I'm thankful for right now because it's going to help me sell this. Nodding towards the fire, I sniffle like I'm fighting not to cry and say, "Still in there. I couldn't get him out." It takes all I have not to let my gaze drift over Angelo's shoulder where Teagan is sneaking up behind him. Just as Teagan is about to wrap his arms around Angelo's neck in a choke hold, he steps on a dog toy that lets out a loud squeak. *Where in the hell did that thing come from?* I don't have time to dwell on it because the noise is enough to draw Angelo's attention. Angelo whips around and smacks Teagan in the face with the butt of the gun sending him stumbling back but Teagan doesn't go down.

Before Teagan can come after Angelo again, Angelo turns to face me and screams, "You lied to me," then he aims the gun at me and pulls the trigger. Fiery pain lights up my lower belly, my leg, and my arm. The last thing I hear is an inhuman roar as Teagan shifts into his bear before everything goes black.

I don't know how long I'm out for but when I come to, I'm in a hospital bed with machines beeping and Teagan asleep in the chair at my side wearing a hospital scrub top that's being stretched to its limits and grey sweatpants that show his ankles and his package because they're at least a size too small.

His hair is disheveled like he's spent a lot of time running his fingers through it. Suddenly, Teagan startles awake and looks around as if expecting a threat. When he doesn't see any, he relaxes and lets his attention turn towards me. Seeing me awake, his face lights up with a huge smile and he exhales a sigh of relief. "Thank the gods. I'm so happy to see you awake, *helkini*. You had me so worried."

Brows furrowing, I question, "How long was I out?"

"About eight hours. You had surgery to remove the bullets and they expected you to be awake about an hour after you were brought back to the room. You not waking when they said you would, scared the shit out of me. Almost as much as seeing you get shot did." Teagan's eyes fill with tears, and I reach out to take his hand.

Squeezing it reassuringly, I tell him, "Hey, I'm fine *vozlyublennyy*. I'm here and I'm fine."

Teagan sniffs and nods. "You almost weren't though. You took eight bullets. Seems luck was on our side or Angelo just had terrible aim because while the bullets did some damage, they missed everything vital."

Holy shit. "I know. It could've been really bad. What happened after I passed out?"

Teagan winces and squeezes the back of his neck as a blush creeps up his cheeks. "I may have shifted and ripped Angelo to shreds then had to face all the first responders naked as a jaybird and covered in blood because they heard the shots and decided it was time to come help despite the possible risks."

The blush on his face deepens and he looks away, like he finds the wall more fascinating than what expression might be on my face. "I'm pretty sure some of the neighbors saw me too but I'm choosing not to think about that right now because if I do we'll have to move. I don't want to have to see the little old lady across the street watering her petunias watching me come out of the house or mowing the lawn and wonder 'is she thinking about the time she saw me naked after I ripped that guy apart'? I mean, I know we're shifters and nudity comes with the territory but something about the elderly seeing it just feels wrong and creeps me out."

Biting my lip, I try my hardest not to laugh but it doesn't work. Still refusing to look at me, Teagan gives me the middle finger which only makes me laugh harder. I'm thankful my healing abilities have kicked in because I'd be in serious pain right now if they hadn't.

When I finally calm down and Teagan has turned his attention back to me, he says sadly, "The house is a total loss. It was fully engulfed by the time the firefighters got water on it. All they could do was contain it, so it didn't spread to the other houses."

Squeezing his hand again, I say, "It's okay. My friend and bandmate Altair can magically recreate it and everything inside if we want to continue with our plan to remodel it from the way it was, or we can just have him recreate our personal belongings and get someone to build us a new house exactly the way we want it."

Teagan shakes his head at that and says, "No, I was really looking forward to making the place ours together so if Altair can recreate it the way it was, that's what I want to do."

"Then that's what we'll do. I'll use the hospital phone to ask Altair to meet us at the ruins of the house and we'll go from there. Now, what do I have to do to get out of here because I'm ready to go so we can start the rest of our lives."

With a chuckle, Teagan leans over and pecks a kiss to my lips. "I'll go find a doctor."

As he leaves the room, I lean back against the pillows with a sigh of relief. *It's finally over*. I'll never have to worry about Angelo again. While I hate that things had to end this way, I'm glad to be rid of him.

Now I can look forward to the future with Teagan and not have to wonder 'what if'. I feel like a weight has been lifted from my shoulders and I can't wait to see what the future holds for Teagan and me. As long as we have each other we can take on anything. Just like the song says, nothing's gonna stop us now and I'm going to enjoy every minute.

Teagan

Epilogue

Halloween – One Year Later…

"Come on, *vozlyublennyy*, we're going to be late! You can test out the new toys Ever sent you later," Alaric shouts up the stairs at me. Rolling my eyes, I put the box I just opened away and head for the stairs. I'm already dressed for the costume party we're going to, I just wanted to see what was in the box before we left.

"I'm coming! Hold your horses, *helkini*." Heading downstairs, I smile when I see Alaric waiting for me in a skintight leather outfit I'm looking forward to peeling off him later. He's playing Catwoman to my Batman. Alaric originally wanted me to be Catwoman but there was no way I could squeeze my big ass into all that skintight leather. Not without a vat of Vaseline, an outfit two sizes bigger and some praying thrown in for good measure. First, we're going to the costume party at the Blue Moon and then we'll go to pack lands for the annual Howl-a-thon potluck, trunk or treat, and pack run. We don't have any kids joining the fun this time around but now that our house is finished I'm hopeful that we will in the future.

I'm in no hurry though. Alaric and I have all the time in the world to start a family. I'm content with it being just us for now especially since there's at least one or two nights a week that I wake up screaming the house down because I've had a nightmare of the night Angelo shot him. I'm seeing someone about it and things have been getting better but I'm not quite there yet. Seeing him on the ground, his blood pooling around him is a permanent image etched onto my soul. I'll never forget it but I'm hoping with time, I won't have nightmares about it.

Alaric has had his share of issues too. For a while there, he wouldn't even look at or touch any packages we had delivered to the house and the sound of a dog squeaky toy still makes him flinch with the memory of being shot. So, I don't think we'll be getting a puppy anytime soon even though we both want one. Other than that, we're doing pretty well. We both still do our jobs. Alaric travels to me by portal when I have to be away for an extended period of time and when he can't come, I go home to him instead. Once we have kids, the routine we have will likely change but for now the arrangement works for us. With Angelo gone and all the labs now fully dismantled, we've settled into a life of peace. One everyone around us needed, not just me and Alaric.

I'm sure sometime down the line something else will happen to shatter our peace because that's life and she throws a mean curveball every now and then. But until then, I'm going to enjoy this peacefulness and be ready to fight come what may. Just like everyone else.

Alaric says, "Are you going to stare at me all day or are we going to get a move on?"

Barking out a laugh, I hop off the last stair and peck a kiss to his cheek. "Someone's bossy today."

Alaric growls. "I'll show you bossy."

Purring at him, I say, "Looking forward to it. You know I love it when you get all riled up."

He shakes his head with a smile and nods toward the door, "Come on, horndog, let's go."

Giving him a two-fingered salute, I tell him, "Sir yes sir," and walk out the front door. As I pass by him, he slaps my ass making me laugh.

Alaric grumbles, "You're lucky I love you," and I smile.

"Yes I am, and I love you too. Now let's make like a tailfeather and shake it. We don't want to be late."

I hear him snort a laugh behind me and say, "That makes no sense whatsoever."

He's right, it doesn't but he gets my point, nonetheless. Hopping in on the passenger side of his truck, I wait for him to start the engine before saying, "To the party Jeeves!"

With a chuckle, he tells me, "You're a nut," and backs out of the driveway.

"I know but you love me anyway."

"Indeed I do, *vozlyublennyy*. Indeed I do."

The End

Thank you so much for reading Alaric and Teagan's story and I'm super sorry about the delay with this release. Like it's been known to happen, life got in the way, but it's finally finished, and I sincerely hope you enjoyed it. Keep an eye out for my next book coming soon.

Alaric's Playlist

Head Over Boots – Jon Pardi

Addicted to Pain – Alter Bridge

Bad Habits – Ed Sheeran

Teagan's Playlist

Heartache Medication – Jon Pardi

Get Through This – Art of Dying

Shivers – Ed Sheeran

Acknowledgements

I want to thank my parents for supporting me no matter what I do and tolerating me when I get in the zone of writing and ignore them completely. By tolerating, I'm really saying thanks for putting up with my shit. You have no idea how much that means to me. I love you guys. I want to thank Lisa Oliver, one of my favorite authors for encouraging me to write the story speaking in my head instead of forcing myself to stick to a different stereotype and for being an amazing friend I can bounce crazy ideas off of.

I want to thank Jemma Brown for designing such amazing covers for me. I thank the readers for taking the time to read a story from an unknown author like me when I was first starting out. I want to thank my characters for coming to me when I was at a loss as to what to write/do next. Last, of all I want to thank all the musicians out there for playing their music and inspiring me.

About the Author

Well, Ezra isn't my real name obviously, but I liked the name, so I decided to use it. I live at home with my four dogs and one cat. I started out writing hetero romance novels, but it wasn't where my heart lied. I adore all things paranormal, and M/M is by far my favorite genre, so I decided to start writing Paranormal Romances. There's a guaranteed happy ending with each of my books even if it may take some time for my guys to get there. I love each character on the page as if they were my own children.

It sounds weird but that's how I feel about them. I've been writing for as long as I can remember but only started actively pursuing it as a career in 2014. Since I published my first book in 2014, I have written and released multiple books with many more to come. My current list of projects is longer than my arm, so I look forward to writing and creating new stories for my readers to enjoy.

Standalones (M/F) *No longer available

Playboy

The Crimson Deceit

Don't Fear the Reaper

The Boy Next Door

Standalones (M/M)

Paying for Love

Law of the Irish

Practical Ghosters

Abominable What-A?

The Cursed Prince

A Raven Walks Into A Bar *Spin-Off*

The Surgeon's Instant Family *Spin-Off*

Not A Snowball's Chance in Hell

Accidental Valentine

Poke His Bear

A Silver Reckoning

Admirer's Halloween *Spin-Off*

The Warden's Easter Trap

The Keeper's Lost Love

Asphalt Bay Pack Series (M/M)

An Alpha for the Demigod

The Enforcer's Secret Vampire

The Beta's Poison Bite

Taming the Feral Tiger

The Doctor's Demon Prince

The Leopard's Twin Troubles

The Warlock's Beautiful Bird

The Demon's Gruff Councilman

The Councilman's Miniature Companion

The Vampire's Special Grizzly *(You just finished it!!)*

The Four Horsemen Collection (M/M)

The Four Horsemen

Azazel

Sen

Taz

The Graveyard Shift (M/M)

The Mortician

The Caretaker

The Director

The Florist

The Mistake *Spin-Off*

The Driver

The Ghost

Venetian Hills (M/M)

The Alpha's Master

The Second's Cursed Mate

The Beta's Second Chance

The Panther's Favorite Bully

The Demon's Mythical Birds

Risqué Business (M/M)

Be My Prince

Seeking Rayne

The Lion's Crown

Ashes of Phoenix

Paranormals of Rockydale (M/M)

Misunderstanding His Mate

The Friendly Ghost's New Beginning

Forbidden Loves (M/M)

All is Fair in Love and War

The Submission Trilogy (M/M)

The Hybrid's Submission

The Wolf's Hybrid Dom

The Hybrid's Dominant Mate

Furry Tails (M/M)

Sugar and Spice

Crimson and Clover

Watson and Sherlock

Snow and Hail

Diary of a Hitman (M/M)

Blood and Bullets

Past and Poison

Love and Lethal

Planet Xenos (M/M)

The Heir's Vampire Guardian

Boxsets (M/M)

Asphalt Bay Pack Vol. 1

Asphalt Bay Pack Vol. 2

The Graveyard Shift Vol. 1

Venetian Hills Vol. 1

Upcoming Releases:

Titles Subject to change

Death and His Necromancer—TBA

The Artist's Prickled Fancy -TBA

Contact the Author

You can find me on Facebook, MeWe, Twitter, and on my website.

Facebook: Ezra Dawn Author or Ezra's Book Groupies

MeWe: Amanda Ezra Ezra Dawn or Ezra's Asphalt Baywatchers

Twitter: @graveshadowcrow

Website: www.ezradawnauthor.com

I look forward to hearing from you!

Want updates on my new releases, WIP's, and exclusive giveaway opportunities? Sign-up for my newsletter by following this link and filling out the form.

Newsletter: www.ezradawnauthor.com/contact